Ever-Clever ELISA

By Johanna Hurwitz

The Adventures of Ali Baba Bernstein

Aldo Applesauce

Aldo Ice Cream

Aldo Peanut Butter

Ali Baba Bernstein, Lost and Found

Baseball Fever

Birthday Surprises: Ten Great Stories to Unwrap

Busybody Nora

Class Clown

Class President

The Cold & Hot Winter

DeDe Takes Charge!

The Down & Up Fall

"E" Is for Elisa

Elisa in the Middle

Even Stephen

The Hot & Cold Summer

Hurray for Ali Baba Bernstein

Hurricane Elaine

The Law of Gravity

A Llama in the Family

Make Room for Elisa
Much Ado About Aldo
New Neighbors for Nora
New Shoes for Silvia
Nora and Mrs. Mind-Your-Own-Business
Once I Was a Plum Tree
Ozzie on His Own
The Rabbi's Girls
Rip-Roaring Russell
Roz and Ozzie
Russell and Elisa
Russell Rides Again
Russell Sprouts
School's Out
School Spirit
Spring Break
Superduper Teddy
Teacher's Pet
Tough-Luck Karen
The Up & Down Spring
A Word to the Wise: And Other Proverbs
Yellow Blue Jay

Johanna Hurwitz

Ever-Clever ELISA

illustrated by Lillian Hoban

Morrow Junior Books
New York

Published by Morrow Junior Books
A division of William Morrow and Company, Inc.
1350 Avenue of the Americas, New York, NY 10019

Printed in the United States of America.

1 2 3 4 5 6 7 8 9 10

Library of Congress Cataloging-in-Publication Data
Hurwitz, Johanna.
Ever-clever Elisa/Johanna Hurwitz; illustrated by Lillian Hoban.
p. cm.
Summary: The year Elisa enters the first grade is filled with exciting times
at school and special celebrations at home.
ISBN 0-688-15189-2
[1. Schools—Fiction.   2. Family life—Fiction.]   I. Hoban, Lillian, ill.
II. Title.   PZ7.H9574Ew 1997   [Fic]—dc20   96-31903   CIP AC

For my ever-clever friend
Annette Bauman

Contents

First Grade
1

Election Day
14

Happy Birthday, Elisa
27

Happy Mother's Day
43

The Lost Lost Tooth
58

A Raffle Ticket
70

First Grade

Yippee! Elisa Michaels was in first grade. She was excited to have finally reached this important point in her life. She had gone to nursery school. She had spent a year in kindergarten. Now, at last, she was in a grade with a *number*—just like her big brother, Russell.

Russell was four years older than Elisa, so he had already been in first grade. He had been in second and third and fourth grade too. Now that

1

Elisa had reached first grade, he was all the way up to fifth.

Elisa and Russell had a baby brother named Marshall. He was so little that he had only a couple of teeth and a little bit of hair. Of course, he didn't go to any school at all.

On the first day of first grade Elisa went to school wearing a new outfit and new sneakers. She had a new backpack to carry home any books and papers that she would get at school. And she had a shiny new lunch box.

The classroom looked familiar. Elisa's kindergarten class had visited the first-grade rooms the year before. She remembered the bulletin board and the plants and the shelf of books all along one wall. There had been a bulletin board and plants and a shelf of books in the kindergarten room too.

What made first grade different was the big chalkboard that covered the whole front of the room. Elisa knew that in first grade her new teacher would write on the board and teach her how to read long words.

Standing at the doorway to greet the first

graders was their teacher. "My name is Ms. Lovelace," she told the children.

The teacher's name was beautiful, and she was beautiful too. She had long blond hair that shook whenever she moved her head. Then Elisa noticed something else. Ms. Lovelace had bright and shiny red polish on her fingernails.

Elisa sat in the seat that Ms. Lovelace assigned to her and studied her own nails. They were the same as always. In fact, her nails looked just like Russell's and Marshall's nails. Girls' nails should be different from boys', she realized.

The first day of first grade was very busy. Books were given out to the students, and the routine was explained by Ms. Lovelace. At lunchtime the teacher walked with her students to the all-purpose room, where long tables were waiting for them. Elisa ate her peanut butter and jelly sandwich and drank the milk in her thermos. She talked with the other students at the table.

"I like Ms. Lovelace," she said.

"Me too," said a girl named Sophie.

"Me too," said a boy named Sam.

"She is beautiful," remarked a girl named Amanda.

Elisa looked down at her hands where some grape jelly had dripped from her sandwich. She licked the jelly from her fingers. "I wish I had nail polish," she said.

"Me too," said the girl named Sophie.

"Me too," said the girl named Amanda.

"Nail polish? Yuck!" said the boy named Sam.

In the afternoon Mrs. Michaels was standing outside the building with Marshall inside his baby carriage when Elisa got out of school.

"How was first grade?" asked Elisa's mother.

"Could I get some nail polish?" Elisa asked.

"Nail polish? What do you need that for?" asked Mrs. Michaels. "Are you doing an art project?"

"Not for an art project. For my nails," Elisa explained. How could her mother be so silly?

"You don't need nail polish," said her mother. "I don't wear any."

"That's because you're an old mother," said

4

Elisa. "Ms. Lovelace, my teacher, wears nail polish. I want to wear it too."

It took three days of nagging until Mrs. Michaels broke down and bought a little bottle of pink nail polish and applied it to Elisa's fingernails. On Friday morning when Elisa got to school, she noticed that every single girl in her first-grade class was wearing nail polish now too.

Elisa was proud to have her fingernails resemble those of her teacher, because she liked Ms. Lovelace so much. The teacher smiled at the children often, and she had a lovely voice. When she read stories aloud to the class, it was like listening to a beautiful princess in a fairy tale.

On the second Monday of September, Amanda came to school with a bag of apples for Ms. Lovelace and the class. "I went to the country over the weekend," Amanda explained to the teacher.

"This is a wonderful treat for all of us. Thank you," Ms. Lovelace said. She bent down and hugged Amanda.

Elisa wished she had brought a wonderful treat for everyone too.

The next day Sophie came to school carrying a big bouquet of flowers for Ms. Lovelace. "Oh, how beautiful!" the teacher exclaimed. She bent down and gave Sophie a hug. Then she found a vase for the flowers and put them on her desk.

Elisa wished she had brought flowers for Ms. Lovelace too. She wondered what she could possibly give her teacher to show her how much she liked her.

That evening Elisa's parents were going out to a concert. Elisa watched as her mother got dressed for the occasion. Mrs. Michaels opened her jewelry box and took out some earrings. Elisa looked in the jewelry box and admired the bracelets, pins, and rings that belonged to her mother.

She tried on one of the rings. It was much too big for any of her fingers, and it even slid off her thumb.

"Why don't you ever wear this?" she asked her

mother. The ring had a piece of shiny glass in the middle.

"I used to wear it," Mrs. Michaels explained. "But I discovered that it scratched Russell when he was a baby. And of course I didn't want to scratch you or Marshall either. So I haven't worn it in a long time."

Elisa watched her mother put the ring back into her jewelry box.

"When you get bigger, I'll give you one of these rings," said Mrs. Michaels. "In fact, some-day all my jewelry will belong to you."

Elisa smiled. She would love to be able to wear all the jewelry when she got older.

Then Elisa got an idea. She would take the ring with the glass in the middle and bring it to school for Ms. Lovelace. She wouldn't *give* the ring to Ms. Lovelace. She would lend it to her. And after Ms. Lovelace was finished borrowing it, Elisa could just put it back.

Elisa imagined how beautiful it would look on her teacher's hand. She also imagined Ms.

Lovelace bending down and giving her a hug.

So that evening while the baby-sitter was busy with Marshall, Elisa removed her mother's ring from the jewelry box. The next morning at school she took the ring out of her pocket and presented it to Ms. Lovelace.

"This is for you," she said. She was about to add "to borrow," but at the very last moment the words didn't come out of her mouth. It wasn't very nice to give someone a gift and tell her she had to give it back.

"Elisa!" exclaimed Ms. Lovelace. "I can't take this from you."

"Yes, yes," Elisa insisted. "It's for you."

"Where did you get this? Did you find it? Does it belong to your mother?"

"It was my mother's," Elisa admitted. "But she doesn't wear it anymore. And she said when I grow up, she is going to give her jewelry to me. So you can have it."

"I will wear it just for now," said Ms. Lovelace. "Then I will give it back to your mother at the end of the day."

Elisa hoped that Ms. Lovelace would like the ring so much that she would decide to keep it. The ring looked very pretty on her finger, and it didn't slide off the way it did when Elisa had tried it on.

At dismissal time Ms. Lovelace followed her class outdoors. When she saw Mrs. Michaels waiting for her daughter, she went over to her.

"I've been wearing this ring of yours all day," she said, removing the ring from her finger.

"My diamond engagement ring!" Mrs. Michaels gasped, recognizing the piece of jewelry that the first-grade teacher was handing her.

"Elisa lent it to me," said Ms. Lovelace.

"Elisa?" exclaimed Mrs. Michaels in a loud voice.

"I just wanted to give her a present," Elisa said.

"That was so sweet of you," said Ms. Lovelace. "But if you take something from one person without asking if you can give it to another person, that's almost like stealing."

"Stealing?" Elisa's eyes filled with tears. She

10

still didn't know how to read or how to do the hard math problems that Russell said he had learned in first grade, but she had known for a long time that stealing was a very bad thing to do. She started to cry.

"I know she didn't mean to steal," Ms. Lovelace told Elisa's mother.

"I was just borrowing it." Elisa sobbed. "Like borrowing library books," she added, wiping her eyes on the sleeve of her sweater.

"It was a mistake," said Ms. Lovelace.

"All right." Mrs. Michaels smiled at Elisa. "No harm done. I've got the ring back."

Ms. Lovelace bent down to look at Marshall. "What a sweet little sister you have," she said to Elisa.

"Sister?" Elisa stopped crying and looked at her teacher in amazement. "Marshall's not a sister. He's my brother!"

"Oh, dear." Ms. Lovelace laughed. "I made a big mistake. Just like you."

Elisa and her mother laughed too. Imagine thinking Marshall was a sister!

* * *

Mrs. Michaels's ring was returned to the jewelry box and Elisa promised never, never, never to take anything out of the box again without her mother's permission. Even if someday all the contents of the jewelry box would belong to her.

Then one day, just a few weeks later, Ms. Lovelace came to school wearing a ring of her own. In fact, she had a big announcement to make to her class.

"In June, when school is over, I am going to get married," she told them.

"Will you have a husband?" asked Amanda.

"Yes."

"Will he be your daddy?" asked Sam.

"No."

"Will you live happily ever after?" asked Sophie.

"Yes, yes, yes," said Ms. Lovelace. She looked prettier than ever that day. Elisa was sure it was because of the ring.

When school was over, Ms. Lovelace followed

the children outdoors and ran to talk to Mrs. Michaels. "I just had to tell you the news," she said. "When my boyfriend heard that one of my students had given me a diamond ring, he didn't want to be shown up by a first grader. The next thing I knew, he gave me this!"

Mrs. Michaels gave Ms. Lovelace a hug. "I hope you'll be very happy," she said.

"Oh, I will," said the teacher. "And it's all because of Elisa."

"Probably not," said Mrs. Michaels.

"I'll never know," said Ms. Lovelace. But she bent down and gave Elisa a big hug and a kiss. It made Elisa feel happily ever after all the way till bedtime.

Election Day

It was a Tuesday morning in November, and
school was closed.

"This is election day," Mrs. Michaels reminded Elisa when she sat down for breakfast.
"School is closed today."

"Yahoo!" Russell shouted. He helped himself
to a second slice of toast. "No school!"

"Russell," Elisa said, looking puzzled, "I
thought you liked school."

"Are you crazy?" Russell asked his sister. "No one likes school."

"I like school," Elisa said.

"That's because you're a girl," said Russell. "Girls always like school. Boys hate school."

Elisa turned to her father, who was finishing a cup of coffee. "When you were a little boy, did you hate school?" she asked him.

Mr. Michaels smiled. "I think I *said* I hated to go to school. That's what boys always tell one another. But the real truth is that I liked school."

"So there," said Elisa to Russell. "Not all boys hate school." She wondered if Russell secretly liked school too.

"I'm off," said Mr. Michaels. He bent down to kiss Marshall, who was rubbing a slice of buttery toast all over the tray of his high chair. He kissed Elisa, and he kissed her mother. "So long, Russ," he said, and he rubbed the top of Russell's head.

Russell always said he hated kissing. Maybe he secretly liked kissing, Elisa thought. Big brothers weren't always easy to understand.

"What are we going to do today?" Elisa asked her mother.

"Well, Russell is going over to play with Kenny," she said.

"Can we go to the library?" Elisa asked. She had finished all her library books.

"Not today," said her mother. "The library is closed because it's election day."

Elisa frowned. "Why is everything closed just because of election day?" she asked.

"It's a kind of holiday," Mrs. Michaels explained as she took the toast away from Marshall. He had started rubbing it on his head.

"Do we get presents?" Elisa asked hopefully.

"It's not that kind of holiday," her mother said. "It's the day everyone goes to vote. This year we're voting for a new mayor. Some years we vote for a president or a senator."

"Well, if kids are too little to go to vote, why are schools closed?" It didn't make any sense to Elisa. It didn't sound like a very good holiday to her.

"The voting is done in the school buildings.

And I suspect schools are closed because so many people are coming and going in the building all day," said Mrs. Michaels.

"Just be happy," Russell told Elisa. "We don't have holidays every week. I won't have any homework tonight," he said.

"I like homework," Elisa reminded him.

"Sure you do," Russell said. "You get such baby homework—cutting pictures out of magazines and stuff like that. You don't have to do math problems or write reports like I do."

"Elisa, you and Marshall will be coming with me when I go to vote," Mrs. Michaels reminded her daughter. "You can watch me vote."

"Goody," said Elisa. She didn't remember ever seeing her mother vote.

"Big deal," said Russell. "That's about as exciting as watching the TV when it's turned off."

Elisa frowned at Russell. He still liked to treat her like a baby. But how could she be a baby if she was Marshall's big sister?

"Better go wash your face and hands," Mrs. Michaels told Russell. "Kenny is expecting you,

17

but he won't recognize you with that strawberry jam on your chin."

Just then the telephone rang. Mrs. Michaels took Marshall from the high chair and carried him with her as she went to answer the phone. A moment later she called to Elisa.

"It's Mrs. Chu," she said. "She's inviting you to go and play with Annie and stay for lunch too."

"Yippee!" Elisa shouted. She loved going to play with Annie, but nowadays they didn't go to the same school, so she didn't see Annie as often as she used to.

Then Elisa thought of something. "If I go to play with Annie, then I can't go with you when you vote."

"You can't do everything. You'd probably have more fun playing with Annie," her mother said.

Elisa didn't know what to decide. She liked playing with Annie, but she also liked the idea of going to watch her mother vote.

"Tell you what," said Mrs. Michaels. "Daddy wasn't planning on voting until after supper. You could go with him if you want."

"Really? At night?" asked Elisa. That would be even more fun than going during the daytime.

"Sure," said her mother.

So Russell went off to play with Kenny, and Elisa went off to play with Annie. She had a good time with Annie, but she was still looking forward to the evening, when she would go to vote with her father.

After supper, while Russell was watching television and Mrs. Michaels was putting Marshall to bed, Elisa put on her warm jacket.

"Don't you want to come with Daddy and me?" she invited Russell.

"You've got to be kidding," said Russell.

"It's just you and me, kiddo," said Mr. Michaels, smiling at his daughter.

They rode down in the elevator of their apartment building and went out into the street. Elisa held her father's hand as they walked. She liked walking in the dark with him, and she looked around as they went. All the stores were bright with lights. She couldn't believe so many people did their shopping at night.

They walked to Elisa's school, where the voting was taking place. It seemed funny to be going to school at seven o'clock at night.

Bright lights shone from every window of the building. Even though Elisa went there five days a week, it looked very unfamiliar at night. But inside the lobby she felt right at home. Elisa showed her father the row of drawings that were hanging on the wall. They had been made by some of the students. She was sorry that none of her pictures was there.

There was a sign with an arrow pointing where to go. They went down the steps to the gym. There along one side of the room Elisa saw the voting booths. They looked like tiny rooms with curtains across their fronts.

There was a long table with people sitting at it and signs indicating A–K, L–R, S–Z. There were lines of people waiting in front of each sign.

"Where do you think I should go?" Mr. Michaels asked his daughter.

Elisa puzzled over the answer. Then she got it. "In the middle," she announced.

"Good for you," said Mr. Michaels as he and Elisa stood at the end of the middle line. "I think they're doing a good job teaching you in this school."

Mr. Michaels nodded to a couple of people he recognized. Elisa wondered if they were surprised to see someone her age out at this hour of the night. She didn't see any other children around at all.

There was a police officer walking around the room. He smiled at Elisa, and she smiled back at him.

"The way it works," Mr. Michaels explained to his daughter, "is that I'll go into one of those voting booths, pull the curtain, and vote. In our country we have a secret ballot, and that's why there is a curtain—to give privacy."

"Can I go inside with you?" Elisa asked. She had just seen a woman coming out from one of the booths, and she wanted to see what it looked like inside.

"I'll ask," her father said. "I don't see why you couldn't."

21

The person ahead of them moved toward the voting booth, and Mr. Michaels gave his name to the man sitting at the table. He turned the pages in a big book and then asked Elisa's father to sign his name.

"May I bring my daughter inside the booth with me?" Mr. Michaels asked.

The man took off his glasses and looked at Elisa. "How old are you, little lady?" he asked her.

"Six and a half," Elisa told him proudly.

"Wow," the man said. He seemed impressed. "And who are you voting for?"

"I can't vote," said Elisa. "I'm not old enough for that." She thought for a moment. "But if I could vote, I'd vote for my daddy."

The man laughed at her answer. "Sure," he told Mr. Michaels. "Take her inside if you want. It's a good lesson in democracy."

Elisa stood next to her father, waiting their turn to go into the voting booth. The man nodded at them. "Next," he said.

Mr. Michaels and Elisa went into the booth. It was very tiny. "Now watch," Mr. Michaels

instructed his daughter. "I pull this lever, and the curtain closes." As he said it, he did it, and suddenly the little booth seemed even smaller as the curtain moved to shut them inside.

"As soon as I finish pulling those little levers, which show the names of the people I'm voting for, I'll pull the big lever again, like this." Mr. Michaels pulled on the lever, and at once the curtain opened again.

"Next," the man called to a woman waiting her turn to vote.

"Wait a minute," Mr. Michaels said. "I didn't vote yet."

"What do you mean you didn't vote?" the police officer standing nearby asked Mr. Michaels.

"I was just showing my daughter how the voting works by pulling on the lever to open the curtain. I didn't actually vote for anyone yet."

"I'm afraid you lost your vote," the police officer said, shrugging.

"Lost my vote?"

"Yep. It happens at least once at every election. Someone goes in and out and doesn't actually make a choice. But when you reopen the curtain, it counts as a vote."

"Oh, well." Mr. Michaels sighed. "I don't think my candidate had a chance anyhow."

"You never know," said the police officer. "Some elections are very close."

"How could you lose your vote?" Elisa asked her father as they walked home again. "I didn't even see it."

"It's a bit complicated to explain. But the system is set up so it's one man, one vote, and if I entered the booth a second time to try to vote, it would look as if I had two votes."

"What about women?" Elisa wanted to know.

"What about them?" asked Mr. Michaels.

"You said one man, one vote."

"Correction," said her father. "One citizen, one vote. Except when the citizen is careless as I was. Or except when the citizen is lazy and stays home and doesn't even go to vote."

"I'll never be lazy," Elisa assured him.

"And I'll never be careless again. I hope," Mr. Michaels said.

"Be careful if you take Marshall with you when he gets big," Elisa said.

"Absolutely," her father agreed.

He looked down at his daughter. "Are you cold?" he asked.

"No," said Elisa. "Are you?"

"No," he told her. "So how do you feel about stopping for an ice-cream cone?"

"I'd feel happy," Elisa reported.

"All right. Let's do it," said her father.

So even though election day wasn't a big holiday with presents, Elisa stayed up late and learned about voting and got a chocolate chip ice-cream cone. It was a special day after all.

Happy Birthday, Elisa

Elisa liked to count. Sometimes it seemed as if she counted everything in the world. When she went shopping with her mother, she counted the number of grapefruits piled in the fruit display. Then she counted the oranges and the apples too.

When she went walking with her father, she counted the number of red cars they saw driving along the street. She counted the number of bald men she saw, and she counted the number of women wearing hats.

She counted Marshall's teeth. There were four. She counted Russell's friends. Six. She counted the number of peas on her plate at suppertime. She was all the way up to seventeen when Mrs. Michaels began to scold.

"Elisa, stop playing with your food. Everything will get cold if you don't hurry up."

"I don't care. I like cold peas," said Elisa. Now she had to start counting all over again.

Elisa counted the number of floors in their apartment building where the elevator could stop. Nine floors if you counted the basement.

"The basement is not a real floor in our building, because no one lives there," Russell pointed out to her.

"I don't care. The elevator still goes there," Elisa insisted.

One morning as they were eating breakfast, Mrs. Michaels gave Elisa some good news. "It's just two weeks until your birthday."

Elisa was thrilled. "Two weeks!" she said with delight. "One, two. It's my birthday!"

"Two weeks is fourteen days," Russell reminded her.

"Oh," said Elisa with disappointment. Fourteen was a whole lot more than two. Fourteen days would take a long time to come.

"Tomorrow it will be only thirteen days until your birthday," said Mr. Michaels. He was just buttoning his coat before he left for work.

"Let me show you the calendar," Elisa's mother offered. "And then you can start counting backward."

Backward was a new way for Elisa to count. She whispered the numbers to herself as she pointed to them on the calendar page. "Fourteen, thirteen, twelve, eleven, ten..."

Now she had the best thing in the world to count, the number of days until she would be seven years old. As the number of days to the big event grew smaller, Elisa got more and more excited.

One afternoon, a week before her birthday, Elisa walked into Russell's bedroom without knocking on the door. Russell was just sliding something out of his backpack and into the bottom drawer of his chest.

"What's that?" Elisa asked him.

"What are you doing in here?" Russell yelled at her. "I never have a minute of privacy. You're always sneaking into my room. I told you that you have to knock. Can't you remember anything I tell you?"

Elisa walked back toward the door and knocked on it. "What did you put in your drawer?" she asked her brother.

"None of your business," Russell said. "Get out of here."

Elisa might have been upset by Russell's tone, but she was used to it by now. After all, she had lived with him for almost seven years. Besides, she was almost certain that Russell's paper bag contained a birthday surprise for her.

Just to be sure, that evening, when Russell was

taking his bath, Elisa sneaked into his room and opened his bottom drawer. Underneath his sweaters she found the bag. Sure enough, inside was a new coloring book. Russell never used coloring books, but Elisa loved them. She turned the pages, admiring all the pictures. It would be fun to color them. Then she put the book back inside the bag and the bag back inside the drawer. Russell would never guess that she had found the surprise!

Having discovered the gift that Russell was going to give her got Elisa thinking. If Russell was hiding a present for her, maybe there were other presents hidden inside the apartment.

Once the idea was in her head, Elisa had a hard time thinking of anything else.

The very next afternoon she waited until her mother was feeding Marshall, and then she went into her parents' bedroom. She knew she shouldn't open their drawers. But she looked at their big bed. On it was a colorful quilt that hung so low you couldn't see the space between the bed and the floor. Underneath the bed would be a perfect hiding place, she thought.

Elisa got down on her hands and knees and looked under the bed. She found her parents' bedroom slippers, but nothing else. Maybe they hadn't bought her any presents yet, she reasoned.

She got up and looked at the closed door to their closet. Maybe there was a present inside the closet. Elisa rushed over and opened the door. On one side of the closet hung her father's slacks and jackets. On the other side were her mother's skirts and dresses. There was a shelf, but it was too high for her to reach. Then she looked down at the floor of the closet. In one corner, behind her mother's clothing, she discovered a paper shopping bag.

Elisa pulled the bag out of the corner and looked inside. There was a giant-size box of crayons. She opened the box. It had too many colors inside for her to count quickly. There were also two new books and a doll wearing a red hood and cape, just like Little Red Riding Hood. Elisa picked up the doll and discovered that she had no legs or feet. She was a hand puppet! That would be fun to play with, she thought happily.

Elisa carefully put all the items back inside the shopping bag, and she put the bag back into the corner of the closet. Then she closed the door and tiptoed out of her parents' bedroom. She felt very clever to have discovered so many of her presents before it was her birthday.

Elisa kept counting the days backward: five, four, three, two, one.

Finally it was the day she had been waiting for. It was her birthday! When she sat down to breakfast, there was a pile of gift-wrapped presents waiting for her.

"Wait," shouted Russell as Elisa reached for her presents. He picked up his violin and played the "Happy Birthday" song.

"I learned it just so I could play it for you," he told his sister. "And it's the first time I ever played the violin before breakfast."

"Now?" asked Elisa. She was eager to open her gifts.

"Now," said her mother.

Elisa grabbed a flat package first. "I bet this is a coloring book," she said as she ripped off the paper. Sure enough, inside was the coloring book that she had found in Russell's room.

Russell was suspicious. "Were you snooping in my bedroom?" he asked his sister.

Elisa didn't answer. She just reached for the next package. It was also flat. But it felt heavier and harder. "Books," Elisa announced even before she ripped off the paper.

"You must have X-ray vision, just like Superman," commented Mr. Michaels when Elisa guessed the contents of the square package the moment she looked at its shape. It was the box of crayons.

There was just one package left, and even before she opened it, Elisa knew what was inside. She felt very disappointed. A birthday should have surprises, but there hadn't been any surprises at all. She had been very happy when she originally found the gifts, but now she had known just what to expect. There were no surprises at all.

Elisa opened the last package and removed the hand puppet. There was a small surprise, however. Her mother showed her that if she turned Little Red Riding Hood upside down, she disappeared and there was a wolf hand puppet in her place. That was a surprise, but it wasn't quite enough for Elisa.

"Is this all?" she asked.

"All? You got a lot of presents," said Russell. "Count them and you'll see."

For once Elisa didn't feel like counting.

"Actually," said Mrs. Michaels, "there are a few other presents for you to expect. The package from Grandma didn't arrive yet, but I'll bet it comes in today's mail."

"And there's one other surprise coming," said Elisa's father, smiling. "It was too big to hide inside our house. But it's going to be here when you come home from school today."

"What is it?" demanded Elisa, jumping up and down.

Marshall, who had been sitting quietly all this

time, banged on the tray of his high chair. It was as if he wanted to know what the surprise was too.

"If we tell you, it won't be a surprise," said Elisa's mother.

"Do you know?" Elisa asked Russell.

"Yep," he said, grinning smugly. "You'll like it."

All day in school, wearing the paper hat that the birthday child always wore, Elisa wondered about the mystery surprise. "Too big to hide," her father had said. What could be too big to hide?

After lunch Mrs. Michaels and Marshall came to visit in Elisa's class. Mrs. Michaels brought enough little cups of ice cream that each child had one. Everyone got a chocolate chip cookie to eat also.

Ms. Lovelace held Marshall as Elisa and her mother distributed the birthday treats to all the first graders. "Did the surprise come yet?" Elisa asked her mother in a whisper.

Mrs. Michaels nodded her head and smiled.

Elisa could hardly wait to go home. But first the class had to sing "Happy Birthday" and eat the ice cream. There was even a cup of ice cream

for Marshall. He waved his arms happily as the cool dessert was spooned into his mouth.

Finally the bell rang announcing the end of the school day. Elisa removed the paper birthday hat and gave it to Ms. Lovelace. In a few days it would be someone else's turn to wear it.

All the way home Elisa tried to guess what the big surprise was.

"Is it a two-wheel bicycle?" she asked.

"No. You're going to get Russell's when he gets a bigger one on his birthday."

"Is it a horse?"

"Whoever heard of a big animal like that in a city apartment?" asked Mrs. Michaels.

"There's a big crocodile in *The House on East 88th Street*," Elisa reminded her mother. The books about Lyle the crocodile were favorites of hers.

"That's just a made-up story," said Mrs. Michaels. "This is real life."

Elisa had run out of ideas. Luckily they had reached their house.

"What a surprise you're going to get!" said Henry, the doorman, as he helped Mrs. Michaels bring Marshall's carriage into the lobby of the building.

"Do you know what it is?" asked Elisa.

"Yes, I do. Happy birthday, sweetheart," said Henry. "It was only yesterday when you were born."

"No, it wasn't," said Elisa. It didn't seem fair that everyone knew about her birthday present but her. After all, it was supposed to be *her* surprise! Even little Marshall probably knew what it was, but he couldn't speak the words yet.

They got into the elevator. Elisa didn't bother to count the buttons. She was too impatient for that today.

They got off at the fourth floor. It seemed to Elisa that it took longer than usual for her mother to get her key out of her pocketbook and get the key into the lock. But finally the door was open, and Elisa rushed inside.

"Where is it?" she shouted.

"Just keep looking. You can't miss it," her mother called back.

Elisa ran into her bedroom, but there was no big package there. She ran into the kitchen, but there was no big package there. "I can't find it," she wailed.

"I thought you were so good at finding things," said Mrs. Michaels. She was busy taking off Marshall's snowsuit. "Keep looking."

Elisa ran down the hallway and looked in her parents' bedroom. She didn't look under their bed or in their closet. Somehow she just knew the present wasn't there. Next she ran into Russell's room. She didn't open his drawers. A really big surprise wouldn't fit in them. It would have to be in the middle of the floor or on his bed. There was nothing there.

Elisa joined her mother in Marshall's room. "I can't find it," she said.

"Don't give up," said Mrs. Michaels. "Come," she added, picking up Marshall and carrying him from the room. "We'll go together and look everywhere."

"But I already looked everywhere," Elisa protested.

"Everywhere? Every single room in this apartment?" asked her mother.

Elisa began counting aloud. "My room, Russell's room, your room, Marshall's room, the kitchen—" Suddenly she thought of a room that she had missed. She ran into the living room, and there against the wall was the birthday surprise. It didn't have any wrapping paper on it, because it was too big. It wasn't a bike, and it wasn't a horse. It was a piano.

"A piano! A piano!" Elisa shouted with joy. "I've always wanted a piano."

"We remembered, even if you forgot." Her mother laughed. "Now you can begin taking lessons too."

"When it's Russell's birthday, I'll play 'Happy Birthday' to him!" Elisa shouted. She looked at little Marshall. "And I'll play it on your birthday too," she promised.

"That's a great plan," said Mrs. Michaels.

"Look at all the keys," said Elisa, touching

the white and black keys on the piano.

"There are eighty-eight," said her mother.

"That's just like Eighty-eighth Street," Elisa gasped with delight. But just to make sure, she sat down and began to count them right away.

Happy Mother's Day

Mother's Day was coming next Sunday. All the boys and girls in Elisa's first-grade class had been making beautiful cards to give to their mothers. Colin lived with his grandmother, so he was going to give his card to her.

Ms. Lovelace read a story to her students about the most beautiful mother in the world. Then there was a class discussion about all the important and wonderful things that mothers do.

"They take us places," said Kimberly.

"They cook our food," said Jenny.

"They do the laundry," said Sam.

"They love us," said Elisa.

Ms. Lovelace smiled and nodded her head at each answer. "You are all right," she said. "Mothers do so many things for us. That is why we have a special holiday once a year to thank them for all that they have done."

Elisa looked down at the card that she had made. She knew her mother would like it. But she wished that she could think of something else to give her on her special day.

"When I was young, I used to bring my mother breakfast in bed on Mother's Day," Ms. Lovelace told the first graders.

"Was she sick?" asked Sophie.

"No, no," said Ms. Lovelace, laughing. "I brought her breakfast in bed so she didn't have to get up and do any work."

"My mother said if you eat in your bed, you'll

get crumbs and make a mess," said Sam.

"Yes. If you're not careful, you would make a mess," agreed Ms. Lovelace. "But my mother was very careful. She didn't make any crumbs. And she enjoyed staying in bed late one morning during the year."

Elisa thought about what her teacher had said. Her mother got up very early every morning. In fact, Elisa couldn't remember ever waking up before her mother. Each morning when she got out of bed, her mother was already in the kitchen, cooking food or feeding Marshall. Wouldn't it be nice if her mother could stay in bed late just once?

Elisa began to plan how she could bring her mother breakfast in bed. Maybe Russell would help her, she thought.

"That's a silly idea," said Russell when Elisa told him her plan. "I don't know how to make coffee. And neither do you. Besides, you're not allowed to turn on the stove."

"We could give her things that don't need

cooking," said Elisa. "We could give her orange juice and cornflakes."

"What's special about that?" asked Russell. "I'm going to buy her a present. I've got some money in my bank."

Elisa had a bank too. It looked like a rooster, and there was a slot in his head to put coins in. There was a place in his stomach that opened up so you could remove the money. Elisa knew there were very few coins inside the rooster. She wouldn't be able to buy anything much for her mother.

The Friday before Mother's Day, Elisa was still thinking about what she could possibly do to make the coming occasion special for her mom. That afternoon, when she was returning from school, she met her friend Nora in the lobby of their building. She didn't know it at the time, but Nora was going to help Elisa solve her problem.

"My mother and I are going to bake some brownies this afternoon. Would you like to come and help?" said Nora.

"Oh. Could I?" Elisa asked her mother. Nora Resnick and her brother, Teddy, were older than Elisa and Russell. But they were still good friends. Nora said that she could remember when Elisa was born. Elisa couldn't remember that, so she didn't really believe that Nora could remember it either. But she loved to spend time with her big friend. And baking would be so much fun.

Mrs. Michaels said it was fine for her daughter to visit Nora. So Elisa remained on the elevator when her mother and Marshall got off. They went all the way up to the seventh floor, where Nora lived.

As they were getting all the ingredients together, Elisa realized that one of the great things about having such a grown-up friend (Nora was twelve years old!) was that she knew so much. Maybe she could help Elisa plan a Mother's Day surprise.

"I want to bring my mother breakfast in bed on Sunday," Elisa explained to Nora. "But I can't cook coffee or eggs or anything. And Russell says that cornflakes aren't special enough for Mother's Day."

"Your mother will think anything you give her is special," Nora reassured Elisa.

"Even cornflakes?"

"Even cornflakes."

When Nora's mother came into the room to help the girls, Elisa didn't say anything more about Mother's Day.

Mrs. Resnick showed Elisa how they were melting baking chocolate together with butter for the brownies. When the mixture cooled, they added four eggs and sugar and vanilla. Then they added flour and nuts. It was amazing how all those things when mixed together and baked would turn into brownies.

While the brownies were baking, Nora and Elisa played a few rounds of tic-tac-toe. Russell had taught it to his sister, and they played it from time to time. For some reason, whenever she played with Russell, Elisa *always* lost. It didn't matter if she made the crosses or the circles. It didn't matter if she went first or second. She never seemed to win. But playing with Nora was a lot of fun. They played six games of tic-tac-toe. Nora won three times, and Elisa won three times. Maybe she'd be able to beat Russell when she got home, she thought.

As they made their marks on the paper, the chocolate smell of the brownies filled the air.

Mrs. Resnick took the pan of brownies from the oven. She didn't cut them until they cooled a bit. "I don't think you should eat a brownie now," she said to Elisa. "It's getting too close to your suppertime. I'll wrap one up, and you can have it after supper."

The chocolate smell was so good it was hard to wait to have the taste of it inside her mouth. But Elisa knew that Mrs. Resnick was right.

It was as she was going downstairs in the elevator to her own apartment that Elisa suddenly knew what she could do for Mother's Day. What could be better than a brownie for breakfast? The brownie was made with eggs and butter and flour and nuts. Those were all good things. If she put the brownie away, she could give it to her mother.

So when Elisa was back in her apartment, she hid the brownie inside her bottom drawer underneath some of her clothing. She didn't tell Russell. He'd probably want to eat the brownie himself.

However, she did challenge him to a game of tic-tac-toe. Despite her success playing with Nora, she lost four games in a row to her brother.

On Saturday Elisa opened her drawer and peeked at the brownie. She opened the wrapper and took a tiny crumb to taste. She wouldn't want to give it to her mother if it didn't taste good. Happily the brownie tasted wonderful. It was hard to resist taking another little pinch of it. But Elisa quickly rewrapped the cake and put it back in her drawer.

When she went to bed on Saturday evening, she suddenly realized that if she didn't wake up before her mother in the morning, her whole surprise would be spoiled. She didn't want to find her mother all dressed and in the kitchen when she got up. Her mother wouldn't want to get back into bed with her clothing on.

As Elisa fell asleep, she thought about how she would have to make every effort to wake before her mother.

In the middle of the night she turned over in bed and woke up. She remembered that this was going to be Mother's Day. Even though it was dark, Elisa got out of bed. It was very quiet in the apartment. That meant her mother was still in bed.

There wasn't a clock in her room, and she wasn't very good at telling time anyhow. Still, she removed the brownie from her bottom drawer and tiptoed into the kitchen. Luckily she was tall enough now to turn on the wall switch for the kitchen light. The kitchen clock showed the hands on the seven and the six. It was seven-thirty, Elisa thought. That's when she usually woke up. Wasn't she clever to wake up early today!

Elisa rested the brownie on the kitchen table.

Then she opened the refrigerator and removed the large container of orange juice. Next she had to pull a kitchen chair over toward the cupboard so she could reach a drinking glass. The juice container was very heavy, and Elisa spilled some of the juice onto her pajamas and on the kitchen floor as she poured it into the glass.

She stood up on the chair again and found a small plate that was just the right size for the brownie. She unwrapped it and put it on the plate. A couple of crumbs fell off, and she ate them. They were delicious, so she knew her mother would enjoy the brownie. It was a hundred times better than old cornflakes for breakfast!

Elisa remembered the beautiful card she had made for her mother. She tiptoed back into her bedroom and took the card out of her backpack.

With the card under her arm Elisa was able to hold the glass of orange juice in one hand and the little plate in the other. It was good that the door to her parents' bedroom was only half-closed. She kicked it open with her foot.

She was so happy to see that her mother was still sleeping. "Happy Mother's Day!" Elisa shouted in her loudest voice into the dark bedroom.

"What—what's that?" came her mother's voice.

"Who's there?" her father called out in a startled tone.

"It's me!" Elisa shouted happily. "Happy Mother's Day. I brought you breakfast in bed."

"Breakfast in bed? What time is it?" asked Mrs. Michaels, sitting up and reaching to turn on the little lamp near her side of the bed.

"The hands were on seven and six, so it's seven-thirty," Elisa explained. She looked at the clock beside the lamp on the bedside table. Now the hands were on the six and the eight. "I got up first so I could bring you breakfast."

Mrs. Michaels reached for the glass of orange juice. "Elisa," she said, "we're going to have to review telling time with you. It's not even

53

six o'clock. It's only twenty minutes to six."

"That's good," said Elisa. "It means I got here before you got out of bed."

"True," agreed her father as he yawned.

"Elisa, you're all wet!" exclaimed her mother.

"It's just a little juice," Elisa explained. "Here," she said, handing her mother both the card and the plate with the brownie. "A brownie for breakfast. I think that's lots better than cornflakes."

"You're right," said Mrs. Michaels, taking a bite from the chocolate offering. "It's absolutely delicious."

"What's all this noise?" said a voice at the doorway. It was Russell.

"Happy Mother's Day!" Elisa told him.

"It's the middle of the night," he replied.

"No, it's not," Elisa protested. She turned to Russell. "You said we couldn't bring Mommy breakfast in bed because we don't know how to make coffee. But I did it, didn't I? So there," she said with an expression of triumph.

From down the hallway they heard a cry.

"Marshie. Marshie," Elisa shouted, running to the door of her parents' bedroom. "He wants to say good morning," she told her mother.

"Happy Mother's Day," Mr. Michaels said to his wife. "I'll go get the baby, and then I'll make you some coffee."

"I've got a present for you too," Russell told his mother. He ran to his bedroom and returned with a wrapped package. "It's chocolate candies, because I know you like that."

"So do I," said Elisa.

She sat down on her parents' bed. There was her mother and Marshall and Russell. Mrs. Michaels opened her present from Russell. Even though they had not eaten any breakfast, she offered them each a piece of her Mother's Day candy. She held the glass of orange juice so that Marshall could get a sip. He was getting very good at drinking from a cup or a glass these days.

In a little while Elisa's father returned, carrying a cup of hot coffee. "Let's trade," he said to his wife. He took the baby and gave her the coffee.

"Someone spilled something on the kitchen floor," he said. "My feet are all sticky."

"It's just a little orange juice," said Elisa. "Orange juice is good for you."

"It's not good for feet, silly," Russell said. He was busy licking the chocolate off his fingers.

"Happy Mother's Day," Elisa told her mother again.

"Thank you, sweetie," said Mrs. Michaels, leaning over and kissing her daughter on her head. "I won't forget this day all year long."

The Lost
Lost Tooth

When Elisa was only four years old, she traded her new hand-knitted mittens to a girl in her class for a tooth. But that was before Elisa had ever lost one of her own baby teeth.

Now that she was seven years old, Elisa had lost several teeth, and each time the tooth fairy had paid a visit to her bedroom during the night.

"I like getting money from the tooth fairy," Elisa said, wiggling one of her upper teeth.

"There's no such thing as a tooth fairy," said Russell. "Don't you know that yet?"

"Then how come you put your tooth under your pillow last week?" she asked her brother.

"That's a good question!" said Mr. Michaels, who overheard their conversation.

"Well, it works, doesn't it?" asked Russell. "I don't care who took that old tooth of mine. Now that I have a camera, I need lots of money," he pointed out. "Film costs money, and it's very expensive to develop my pictures."

Russell had gotten a camera for his birthday, and he had already filled up half an album with the pictures he had taken. There were pictures of Marshall wearing his new shoes and beginning to walk. And there was a picture of Elisa smiling and missing her two top teeth.

Elisa wiggled her tooth again as she sat down to do her homework. These days she felt very grown-up doing homework almost every afternoon.

"Guess what?" she would announce proudly when she came home from school.

"What?" asked Mrs. Michaels. She never bothered to guess.

"I have two pages of homework."

"Ahammm," Marshall responded. He didn't know what homework was, but he was trying hard to talk these days.

Elisa loved doing her homework. Some days she had to practice making her letters. She had learned how to print every letter of the alphabet in lowercase now. She worked slowly and neatly. Some days she had math work to do. She could add and subtract.

"Wait till you get fractions!" Russell told her. "Wait till you get decimals. Wait till you get percentages."

Elisa didn't know what all those things were. But she refused to let Russell scare her. It would be a long time until she had to worry about whatever fractions were.

Today as she wrote, she pushed at the top tooth, which was beginning to feel looser and looser. She even turned to her doll Airmail, who was sitting on her bed. "I'm going to lose another

tooth soon," she reported happily. "I can feel it."
Now that she was getting so grown-up, Elisa
didn't talk to Airmail as much as she used to.
But sometimes she forgot and confided in her
doll just like in the old days.

When Elisa had finished her homework, she
put all the papers away and went to practice for
her piano lesson the next day. She could already
play several pieces: "Row, Row, Row Your Boat,"
"Twinkle, Twinkle, Little Star," and her favorite,
"Pop Goes the Weasel."

"Hey, Mom," Russell shouted.

Elisa stopped practicing. She could tell from
his tone that Russell had a problem.

"What is it, hon?" Mrs. Michaels called back.

"I left the sheet that my teacher gave us with
the homework questions in my desk at school.
How can I do my homework?"

"You could phone one of your classmates
and ask him to tell you the questions," his mother
suggested.

Elisa smiled. Their mother always knew how
to solve problems. She began practicing again as

Russell went to the phone. It wasn't until supper-time that Elisa learned that Russell still couldn't do his homework. He had called four of his friends: Kyle, Kenny, Bruce, and Jared. Kyle wasn't home. Russell had forgotten that Kenny had been absent from school. Of course he didn't have the sheet of problems. Bruce's phone was busy. And Jared had left his sheet at school too.

After supper that evening Russell tried to call Bruce again.

"Nuts!" he called out. "It's still busy. Why don't they have call waiting at their house? This is important."

"Maybe their phone is broken," said Mr. Michaels. "Or maybe the phone is off the receiver, and they're not aware of it."

Whatever the reason, Bruce was Russell's last hope. And even though he kept trying all evening, he never succeeded in reaching his classmate on the phone.

"What am I going to tell my teacher?" Russell sounded worried.

"I'll write a note to her," said Mrs. Michaels,

"and I'll explain why you didn't do your homework. But you must promise to be more careful in
the future."

Russell looked relieved. And once again Elisa
thought how good their mother was at solving
problems.

It was while they were having supper a few
evenings later that Elisa made an amazing discovery. "I lost my tooth," she shouted. Her tongue
probed the new space in her mouth. "But I don't
know where it is!"

"Did you swallow it?" asked Russell.

Elisa looked worried. The tooth wasn't in her
mouth. It wasn't on her plate. It wasn't in her
hand. She must have swallowed it. She swallowed
again hard. She hadn't even felt the tooth going
down her throat. It must have been mixed up
with the food she was eating.

"Will it chew up my stomach?" she asked,
alarmed.

"No. No. It's like accidentally swallowing a
piece of gum or a hard candy. Don't worry about

it," said her father, smiling at her. "Which one is this now? Number five?"

"No, six," said Elisa, correcting him. Suddenly she had a terrible thought. "I can't put it under my pillow. How will the tooth fairy know that I lost it?"

"Sleep with your mouth open," said Russell.

"Why don't you write a little note and stick it under the pillow?" suggested Elisa's mother.

"That won't work," said Russell. "It's too dark in the bedroom for the tooth fairy to read a note. If there really is a tooth fairy, that is."

"If the tooth fairy has eyes good enough to find a tooth in the dark, then the tooth fairy will be able to read Elisa's note," said Mrs. Michaels, looking at Russell. She sounded very certain about that.

"Yeah. I guess you're right," Russell agreed. He smiled at his parents, and his father gave him a wink.

As soon as supper was over, Elisa sat down and wrote a note. It was good she had learned to make all the lowercase letters so neatly.

She read her note over several times. Then she had another idea.

Dear Tooth Fairy,
I swallowed my tooth. It is not under my pillow because it is inside my stomach.
From,
Elisa M.

She ran to her mother and said, "I wrote my note, but I want you to write one too."

"Why me?" asked Mrs. Michaels. "I didn't lose a tooth."

"I know that," said Elisa. "But remember how you wrote a note for Russell to give to his teacher when he forgot his homework paper at school? That's the kind of note I want you to write. You could explain that it was an accident and that I'll try not to swallow my tooth next time."

"Of course," said her mother. "I'll be glad to do that. Let me just get Marshall ready for bed first."

So Marshall was washed up and put into his pajamas. Elisa watched and tickled his toes and blew kisses at him. He was really the best baby in the whole world, she thought. He smiled at her. He had many teeth now. In fact, for every tooth that Elisa or Russell lost, he seemed to grow one of his own.

"Maybe the tooth fairy gives my old teeth to Marshall," Elisa said.

"No, I don't think so," said Mrs. Michaels. "Every child grows his or her own teeth."

"Okay," said Elisa. She was relieved. She didn't want to deprive her brother of a new tooth just because she had accidentally swallowed it. Besides, Marshall deserved brand-new teeth, not used ones.

Marshall was put into his crib, and the light was turned off in his room. Then Elisa watched as her mother wrote a note to the tooth fairy. It was written in the scribbly-scrabbly way that grown-ups used. Elisa was glad. Even though she couldn't understand it all, it looked important.

Dear Tooth Fairy,

My daughter Elisa accidentally swallowed her tooth while eating supper this evening.

Please be sure to leave a gift under her pillow.

Mrs. Michaels

The tooth fairy must have been able to read in the dark. And the tooth fairy must have understood the situation. Because the next morning when Elisa woke up, she made a wonderful discovery. The two pieces of paper were no longer under her pillow. In their place was a single piece of paper. It was a dollar bill! It was the most money the tooth fairy ever left for a tooth. It made Elisa feel very, very rich.

A Raffle Ticket

On Saturday, just a few days later, Elisa was feeling *super* rich. In one week she had lost a tooth and found a quarter. The tooth fairy had left a dollar under her pillow, and the quarter was lying on the sidewalk the day before as she walked home from school. So now there was one dollar and twenty-five cents in her bank.

"What shall I buy with my all money?" she asked her mother.

"Is it burning a hole in your pocket?" Mrs. Michaels asked.

"How can it burn a hole in my pocket when it's inside my bank?" Elisa wanted to know. She felt the dress she was wearing. "I don't even *have* a pocket today."

"'Burning a hole in your pocket' means you can't wait to get rid of the money. I suggest you just hold on to it. You'll think of something to spend it on before you know it," Mrs. Michaels said.

"Should I take it out of my bank?" asked Elisa.

"No. Then you'll lose it for sure," said her mother.

"But you said I should hold on to it. I can't hold on to it when it's inside my bank."

"Never mind. Leave it safely inside your bank," said Mrs. Michaels. She was busy feeding Marshall some lumpy carrots. He didn't eat mushy food anymore. He was getting big enough to chew on little lumps. But he seemed to spit out as many as he took in.

71

"I don't think he likes that," Elisa said, making a face. "I wouldn't like to eat it."

"You loved it when you were his age," said Mrs. Michaels, scooping up another spoonful and putting it into Marshall's mouth.

"Ahma-ah," said Marshall, smiling so that his little white teeth peeked through the orange mush in his mouth.

"He says it's awful," said Elisa.

"No," said her mother, putting another spoonful into Marshall's mouth. "He just said how much he likes it."

The doorbell rang before Marshall, Elisa, or their mother could say another word.

"I'll go get it," shouted Elisa with delight.

"Don't open the door until you find out if it's someone we know," her mother reminded her.

There was a peephole in the door, but it was too high for Elisa to look through. "Who is it?" she shouted in her loudest voice.

"It's me. Eugene Spencer," the voice on the other side of the door replied.

Eugene Spencer was one of their neighbors. He lived on the fourth floor too, in apartment 4E. It was just down the hallway from 4H, where Elisa and her family lived. Eugene Spencer went to high school, which is where really big kids went to school.

"Wait a minute," Elisa called to Eugene Spencer. She pushed a chair over toward the door, and when she stood on it, she was able to turn the latch. Then she got down off the chair, pushed it out of the way, and opened the door.

"Hi," she said, shyly looking up at him. She hardly ever talked to him. He was very tall and almost a grown-up.

"Elisa? Who's there?" Mrs. Michaels called from the kitchen.

"It's Eugene Spencer," their neighbor identified himself. He walked toward the kitchen, and Elisa followed him.

"I'm selling raffles for my school," said Eugene Spencer. "We're raising money to buy

73

new gym equipment. The raffles cost only a dollar each. And there are really neat prizes. Do you want to buy some?"

"What's a raffle?" asked Elisa.

"It's one of these little tickets," said Eugene Spencer, showing her. "Each one has a number on it. On June first we're going to pick the winning numbers. The winners will get the prizes."

"What are the prizes?" asked Mrs. Michaels as she wiped Marshall's face with a damp washcloth.

"The grand prize is a four-day cruise to the Bahamas for two people," said Eugene Spencer proudly.

"Oh. A cruise!" said Elisa, her voice filled with awe. Then she asked, "What's a cruise?"

"It's a trip on a big boat, and you eat and sleep on the boat for four days," Eugene Spencer explained.

"For a dollar?" Elisa was really impressed.

"Sure, if you have the winning raffle," said Eugene Spencer. "And there are other prizes too.

Second prize is five hundred dollars, and third prize is a video camera."

"I want the cruise," said Elisa. She wasn't sure how much five hundred dollars was, and she didn't know how to work a video camera.

"If you win, you'll get it," said Eugene Spencer.

"You have the makings of a fine salesman," said Mrs. Michaels, adjusting Marshall in his high chair. "In fact, you've convinced me. I'll take two tickets."

"Great," said Eugene Spencer. "I've been selling to everyone in the building. Some people even took five. And Mr. Murphy on the first floor bought ten."

Mrs. Michaels took two dollars out of her pocketbook to give to Eugene Spencer. Elisa rushed off to her room and came back with her bank.

"Here," she said to her neighbor. "I have a dollar in my bank. I want to buy one of your raffles too."

"Great!" said Eugene Spencer.

"Oh, honey," said Mrs. Michaels to her daughter, "I'll give you one of the tickets that I buy. You don't have to spend your own money."

"No," said Elisa firmly. "It's my money, and I want to buy my own ticket. But when I win the cruise, you can come with me," she offered. "Eugene Spencer says it's for two people."

"I don't think I could go with you." Her mother laughed. "Who would look after Marshall and Russell and Daddy?"

"Oh." Elisa hadn't thought of that. "Maybe I'll take Russell," she said.

"I'm just kidding," said her mother. "The chances of winning a raffle are very slight. The reason you buy a raffle ticket is to help a cause. In this case what I'm really doing is giving a donation of money to Eugene Spencer's school. I don't count on winning anything. Nobody ever wins a raffle."

"Mrs. Michaels," said Eugene Spencer with great surprise, "somebody has to win. There's always a winner, and it could be *you.*"

"It could be *me*," said Elisa.

"That's right, it could," said Eugene Spencer.

Mrs. Michaels sighed. "I said you'd make a great salesman someday, but I was wrong. You're a great salesman already."

Eugene Spencer took the two dollars from Mrs. Michaels and the dollar bill from Elisa. In exchange he gave them their raffle tickets. "This is your number," he told Elisa. He pointed to the number in the corner of her ticket: 347. "You're seven years old now, right?"

Elisa nodded her head.

"So this is a real lucky number. Three and four are seven, and you're seven years old!"

"Three-four-seven!" repeated Elisa. She liked the number. "It's a very lucky number," she said. "Besides, there are three children in my family, and we live on the fourth floor, *and* I'm seven years old."

"Well. Good luck!" said Eugene Spencer. He put the money in his pocket and headed toward the door.

"Wait till I tell Russell that we're going on a

cruise," said Elisa. "He'll be very surprised."

"I'll be very surprised too," said her mother.

When Russell came home, he wasn't the least bit impressed by the news at all. "Forget it," he told his sister. "You're never going to win. The only water you're going to see is in the bathtub."

"Somebody has to win," said Elisa, quoting Eugene Spencer. "Besides, I got a lucky number," she told Russell. She showed him her raffle ticket.

"I can't believe you spent a whole dollar for this little piece of paper," Russell said.

"You'll see," said Elisa. "I'm going on a cruise, and just because you're so mean about it, I won't take you. I'll take Daddy with me."

"He can't go off on a cruise, silly. He's got to go to work."

"Then I'll take Nora or Annie Chu or one of my other friends. But not you," said Elisa.

"Oh, I'm so sad," said Russell. "Boo-hoo," he teased, pretending to cry.

"You'll be sorry," said Elisa. She went into her

room and carefully put her raffle ticket away. Airmail was sitting on her bed. No matter who else she invited to come along on the cruise, she knew that Airmail would come too.

Elisa didn't think about her cruise all the time. As the days passed, there was school and piano lessons and practicing her new pieces. Now that it was really spring, the weather was warm enough for playing in the park. It was fun to go on the slides and swings again. And she finally learned how to ride Russell's old two-wheeler. One Saturday evening she had a sleepover date with Annie.

But from time to time she took out her little raffle ticket and studied it. *Winners will be announced on June 1,* it said on the bottom of the ticket.

June 1 was a Friday, and Elisa was at school all day, of course. She would have forgotten about the raffle ticket had she not seen Eugene Spencer in the elevator when she returned home in the afternoon. It was crowded in the elevator with

Eugene Spencer and another big boy and Elisa and her mother and Marshall's stroller with Marshall inside.

Elisa squeezed over next to Eugene Spencer. "Did I win?" she asked him.

"Win what?" asked Eugene Spencer. He had nodded to them when they entered the elevator, but he was busy talking with his friend about a baseball game that they were going to the next afternoon.

"My cruise," said Elisa. "Today's the day that the winners are going to be announced for the raffle."

"Oh, yeah," said Eugene Spencer. "Well, they read the names and the numbers over the PA at school this afternoon. And I don't remember hearing yours."

"Maybe you weren't listening carefully," said Elisa hopefully.

"Elisa," said her mother, "I told you that you shouldn't count on winning a prize."

"But somebody had to win," Elisa reminded her mother.

"Somebody did," said Eugene Spencer's friend. "But I guess it wasn't you. It wasn't me either," he added, looking at her sympathetically.

"I told you you wouldn't ever win the raffle," Russell said smugly while they were waiting for supper to be ready. He was playing a round of tic-tac-toe with Elisa. "But you wouldn't believe me."

"Somebody had to win," Elisa said sadly. "I thought it would be me. The ticket had lucky numbers on it." She made her second circle in a row and held her breath. Maybe, just maybe, she'd beat Russell this time.

"There's no such thing as a lucky number," said Russell. "I can't believe how dumb you can be." He carelessly made a cross in the top corner.

"I'm not dumb," shouted Elisa. She marked her third circle and beat Russell. "And you know what else?" she asked with delight.

"No. What?" asked Russell.

"I'm going on a cruise anyhow."

"You've got to be kidding," said Russell. "What kind of cruise can you go on in the bathtub?"

"Not in the bathtub, smarty. My teacher said my class is going on a trip to the Statue of Liberty, and we're going on a boat. And we're going to eat our lunch on the boat too. So that's just like a cruise. It *is* a cruise!"

"What a wonderful plan," said Mrs. Michaels.

"That's not a cruise! On a cruise you sleep on the boat too," said Russell.

"I could fall asleep on the way to the Statue of Liberty if I wanted to. But I don't want to. So I won't," said Elisa.

"Well. You still were silly to spend a whole dollar for that raffle ticket," Russell told her.

"No. Mommy said that the money is for a good cause," said Elisa. And then she smiled to herself because she had a secret that Russell didn't know. That afternoon in school she had discovered another loose tooth in her mouth. She had a feeling that before very long the tooth fairy was going to be leaving another dollar bill under her pillow. She still had the quarter that she'd found. She would be rich all over again. So there!